AF348706

Mysteries
of the
Mist

Mysteries of the Mist

Published by Gatekeeper Press
7853 Gunn Hwy., Suite 209
Tampa, FL 33626
www.GatekeeperPress.com

Library of Congress Control Number: 2022945214

ISBN (hardcover): 9781662931260
ISBN (paperback): 9781662931277
eISBN: 9781662931284

Mysteries of the Mist

C.A. Rand

gatekeeper press
Where Authors are Family ™
Tampa, Florida

Acknowledgments

Thank you, Gatekeeper Press! I appreciate the hard work and dedication of your staff. They did an amazing job. A special thanks to Aimee, my author manager. You made this process flow smoothly. My deepest appreciation to Danilo, illustrator extraordinaire. Your beautifully crafted illustrations are truly a work of art!

Chapter One

Coralee loved the rich, briny smell of the sea; the jagged, rocky cliffs; and the noisy marine life that frequented the coastline. She had deep affection for her island home with all its legends and folktales, which added to its charm and uniqueness.

Coralee lived near Kingfisher Point, located at the southern tip of Sirena Island along with her mother, father, and older brother. Her family worked for a large commercial fishing company. Her father and brother were among the fishermen who sailed the seas for weeks at a time on large fishing trawlers, returning with a cargo of fresh fish to sell. Her grandpa, now retired, had also worked as a commercial fisherman for many years.

He had recently accepted a job of lightkeeper for the lighthouse at Silver Wing Point on the northernmost point of the island. The lighthouse and small cottage attached to it needed repairs. The place had been vacant for a long time. After a family discussion, it was decided that Coralee would spend the summer at the lighthouse assisting her grandpa with cleaning, cooking—and the best part—decorating the two-bedroom cottage.

With her driver's training completed in the spring, Coralee now had a driver's license. She borrowed the small pick-up truck that was once her brother's. She filled the back of the little truck with clothes, books, journals, and her art supplies. On her way out of town she stopped at several shops to complete the shopping list of supplies her grandpa had asked her to pick up along the way.

With the sandy beaches of Kingfisher Point in her rear-view mirror, she headed north where the landscape changed to rocky shores and wooded inlands. Very few people lived near Silver Wing Point, as the landscape was quite rugged and much of the time the area was cloaked in sea mist.

Lost Lily Lagoon was a few miles south of the lighthouse where her grandpa docked his fishing trawler, the *Ole Scallywag*. There was a fish and tackle shop that also served as the post office and grocery store. Across the street from the docks was the local watering hole, the Seadog Saloon and Café. Dorsea ran the café, and she made the world's best fish chowder and biscuits. Coralee couldn't wait to have a steaming bowl of chowder and biscuits before continuing her journey to the lighthouse.

"Coralee, my aren't you a sight? Why, you get more beautiful every time I see you," chimed Dorsea from behind the café counter.

Dorsea was a portly woman with sea-weathered skin and hair of gold she always wore in a French braid.

"Come have a seat at the counter and tell me all the news of Kingfisher Point."

"Only if you have a bowl of that delicious fish chowder saved for me," joked Coralee.

"You're in luck, this one has your name on it."

MENU

Coralee gave her an update on the happenings at Kingfisher Point and told her that she would be staying at the lighthouse with her grandpa for the summer.

"That's kind of a lonely place for a young girl like you."

"Oh, I have things planned; I have my sketch pad and paints, my novels, and Grandpa needs help getting the cottage put back together. I have a handful of surprises for him. I bought throw pillows and decorations to make it feel homier. It will take most of the summer just to get everything painted and decorated. I'm excited. I love doing this stuff!"

"Quite the 'Suzy Homemaker' you are, Coralee! Just sounds like work to me."

After saying her goodbyes to Dorsea, she continued her journey to the lighthouse.

Chapter Two

From Lost Lily Lagoon to the lighthouse there were no other homes or businesses. Some would say that stretch of road was eerie and gloomy, but for Coralee it was mystical. As a small child she remembered stories of sea fairies, forest nymphs, and mermaids that traveled in the cloak of mist. She would always look for them on this stretch of road hoping to catch a sight of one, but they were particularly good at hiding.

Grandpa's white diesel truck was in the driveway when Coralee turned the corner. This was the first time she had seen the lighthouse and cottage since she was a child. Time and the sea air made it look tired and old. *Well,* thought Coralee, *it will take most of the summer to bring it back to life, but I can see the beauty that lies beneath the scruffy surface just waiting to be exposed.*

Her grandpa Rodman Reel, better known as 'Rigger,' was up on the scaffolding whitewashing the exterior of the lighthouse. He loved this old lighthouse. When he decided to retire, he inquired if the building was still vacant. Told that the property was still for sale, he jumped at the chance to purchase it. He wanted to restore it to its glory days and leave it as an inheritance for his family to enjoy.

Working on this old lighthouse was a labor of love. Oh, how beautiful it was in years gone by, a pristine white cottage and cylindrical tower with bright red roofs. There were flowers and shrubs around the cottage with a small garden on the far side. On a cloudless day when you gazed upon the sea, its boundaries were limitless. You could see freighters and trawlers sailing past and the ever-present seagulls swooping and diving near the coast. With every brushstroke he saw the old girl come back to life.

"Coralee, did you remember to get my supplies in town?" Rigger yelled from the scaffolding.

"Yes, Grandpa! I got everything on the list plus a few surprises I'll show you later."

"Set the paint cans next to the scaffolding, dear."

"I stopped to see Dorsea, and she sent chowder and biscuits for you. Are you hungry?"

"Starving, I'll be right down. Certainly won't pass up chowder and biscuits!"

Coralee unloaded the truck and stacked the supplies on the porch. She then carried her personal items into the front bedroom. There was a twin bed with her grandmother's nautical handsewn quilt on top and a desk with chair under the window that looked out to sea. Opposite the bed, a chest of drawers sat; resting on top was her grandmother's rose-engraved, silver-plated hand mirror, comb, and brush set with a matching silver-plated wall mirror that was a twenty-fifth wedding anniversary gift from Grandpa.

After putting her things away, she joined him in the living room. With evening the damp fog came rolling in, so Rigger gathered firewood and made a small fire in the hearth. They sat and visited.

Grandpa spoke of how her grandmother would have loved to see this old place come to life, and how he missed her since her passing. Coralee was chatting away when she looked up and noticed he had fallen asleep in his recliner. *Hard work and fresh air will do that,* thought Coralee, as she covered him with a blanket and then went to her room to write in her journal at her desk.

It had been weeks of hard work. The lighthouse tower was patched and painted; its windows atop were clean and sparkly. The progress was slow but rewarding.

Coralee had washed all the walls inside the cottage to get them ready for paint. She chose a light blue shade of paint called 'ocean breeze.' It would brighten the interior's dark wood moldings, floors, and cabinets.

But before she started on another big project, she was going to give herself the morning off. It was sunrise and the gulls were making noise below the lighthouse. She followed the winding footpath through the woods for a refreshing morning hike. The lingering cool morning mist felt so good on her skin.

Refreshed and relaxed, she returned to the cottage to fix lunch for herself and her grandpa. Rigger told Coralee he was going to Lost Lily Lagoon to meet up with the locals for a few pints and would return tomorrow. He planned to spend the night in his trawler cabin; it wasn't safe to drive home after drinking in the saloon. Once a month Rigger would go to the Seadog Saloon and meet up with his old fishing buddies.

"Stay off the rocky cliffs, they're not safe!" he warned as he drove away.

You'd think I was a child, thought Coralee. "OK, Grandpa. Have a good time!"

Chapter Three

When Coralee was a little girl, she was a bit of a monkey. She climbed on anything and everything, whether big or small, so these cliff rocks did not scare her.

Grandpa is not here, she brazenly thought, *so how will he know?*

The sun was beginning to set. Coralee took her backpack, which held a sweatshirt, flashlight, first-aid kit (in case she skinned her knee), and her sketchpad.

I'll find a perfect view of the sunset to sketch, Coralee reasoned.

Carefully, and with sure feet, Coralee navigated her way over the jagged cliff rocks, slowly working her way to the black sand beach below. On her journey down the cliff face she stopped to sketch wildflowers growing in between the rocks.

Near the bottom of the cliff something strange caught her eye. There was a wet imprint on one of the rocks. It looked like a handprint, but there was no one else on the cliff. In fact, there was no one within miles of the lighthouse.

How strange, she thought, so she crept down closer to the rock to get a better look.

As she knelt next to the rock, she placed her hand on top of the darkened imprint. The handprint was almost the same size as her hand.

Coralee was puzzled—*how did it get there?* The longer she stared at it the more it faded away with the sea breeze.

As she stood up her foot slipped and knocked a rock loose. It went cascading down the cliff until it hit something at the bottom. She could have sworn she heard a low whimper, but it was hard to know for sure with the surf crashing against the rocks. Coralee stood frozen, not sure if her mind was playing tricks on her, or if she should continue down the cliff to investigate. Stories that her grandfather told her as a child about mermaids and sea fairies were dancing through her mind.

Oh, this is ridiculous, she thought, *I'm at the bottom as it is, I might as well descend to the beach and set my mind at ease.*

Within a few minutes Coralee was standing on the black sand beach in a narrow cove. As the sun had set, she took out her flashlight to look for footprints in the sand. She found none. There were, however, strange indentations that looked like a fish fin dragged across the sand.

Maybe it was something moved across the sand by the waves, she speculated.

As she turned to head back up the cliff, she heard the low whimper again. She scanned the edge of the rocks below the cliff where she had been climbing with her flashlight and saw the tail of what she thought was a marine animal wedged in between a couple large rocks.

Ah, a baby seal is stuck, she thought.

She approached very slowly to not frighten the animal. When she bent down to check for injuries, a section of the tail flapped angrily, and a young girl's head popped up. Coralee was so startled she ran backwards until she fell, her backpack cushioning the fall.

"You're, you're, you're a mermaid," stuttered Coralee. The young mermaid covered her face and whimpered.

"Wait, are you alright? Are you hurt?" inquired Coralee.

The young mermaid continued whimpering. Coralee rose to her feet and slowly approached the girl. She turned her flashlight back on to see if she was stuck or injured.

"It looks like your tail fin is partially stuck under that big rock!" exclaimed Coralee. "That is why you can't move. My name is Coralee, I'll help you. I won't hurt you."

Coralee searched for something to wedge under the rock to lift it up so the mermaid could pull her tail fin out. After searching, she found a sturdy piece of driftwood and worked to pry up the rock just enough to provide space for the mermaid to free herself. As the mermaid pulled out the corner of her tail fin, she rolled over onto the warm, black sand. Coralee grabbed her backpack and flashlight and bent down next to the mermaid's tail.

"I have a first-aid kit. Let me examine your fin to see if there are any cuts."

Coralee gently stretched out the fin and applied an oil salve to the abraded areas. "This is all I have, but it should help it heal and not become infected."

As Coralee turned away to reassemble her first-aid kit and place it in her backpack, the young mermaid slid back into the sea. When Coralee turned around to ask her name, she was gone. She stared out to the horizon, seeing a tail fin slapping the water and then disappearing into the sea.

As Coralee climbed back up the rocky cliff face, she was full of thoughts. *I sure have a lot to write in my journal tonight. I can't tell grandpa. He would be furious that I disobeyed him. I wonder if she'll ever come back. She was so afraid. It's hard to tell but I believe she was close to my age.*

Chapter Four

Mist knew that she was in deep trouble. She only wanted to see the human girl; she could have escaped unnoticed if that rock had not fallen on her tail.

Oh, how her tail hurt, but not as much as it was going to hurt telling her mom where she was and what had happened. She swam furiously to the small cave opening hidden deep in the volcanic sea wall.

As she slid through, she swam quickly along the lava tube to the opening on the other side. This was a haven where her pod of merfolk lived. Here she was protected from the evil Sirens. Her mother's face had a scowl on it as Mist swam towards her.

"Where have you been, my young merling? I've looked everywhere for you!"

"I went for a swim," telepathed Mist sheepishly, "a little adventure is all."

"Mist, you are a defiant merling," scolded her mother. "You do not heed our warnings. Were you seen by a Siren or human?"

"I saw no Sirens, but I accidentally met a human. Sorry, Mom."

"What? Humans only know the ways of the Sirens. That is what their legends and folklore are based on. They do not know our ways, the ways of the Nereus. What did you mean by 'contact'?"

"I was sunning myself near the old lighthouse on the lava rocks when I spotted a young girl. She was climbing down the cliff face. I just wanted to get a quick look at her when a rock fell from above and pinned my tail fin. She came and lifted the rock so I could get free and put oily stuff on my tail. When she turned her back, I slid back into the sea and disappeared.”

“Oh, Mist, you have made things so complicated. You know any interaction with a human must be reported to the Sea Goddess. There are reparations that must be made for the human girl’s kindness. I will telepath her that you are coming. Go to her now!”

The Sea Goddess, Kleenah, was awaiting Mist’s arrival. She was the most beautiful of all the Nereus Mermaids with a lustrous tail of blue and green, glittering hair of spun gold, and eyes the color of emeralds. Kleenah was revered for her kindness and wisdom. Her husband, the Sea God Cronus, was leading a hunting expedition in search of the evil Sirens. *Well*, thought Mist, *at least I don’t have to deal with both.*

As Mist approached Kleenah she bowed her head in respect.

“Come here, little merling, we have matters to discuss. You broke a sacred rule of the Nereus pod,” Kleenah reprimanded. “You put yourself and our pod’s safety in jeopardy. But since this human girl saved your life, you must make amends. Tomorrow morning, under the cloak of fog, you will be escorted by a Nereus warrior back to the black sands below the lighthouse. You will place this moonstone on a rock and use your telepathic powers to call the girl back to the beach and guide her to the stone. Once she picks up the stone necklace, through telepathy, you will inform her of the powers of the moonstone. She is to never reveal what she has seen or the powers of the stone. If she fails to keep the mermaid secret, a fatal curse will fall upon her. If she is ever in danger near or on the sea, she is to hold the moonstone tightly in the palm of her hand and repeat this chant—*‘Mermaids of Nereus, hear my plea, I am in peril, please come save me.*' She'll know we've heard her call as the moonstone will turn from grey to teal. Once you have returned from this task, you will not leave this pod without an escort until you have completed your mermaid rituals. Do I make myself clear, merling Mist?"

"Yes, Goddess," resigned Mist.

Kleenah handed the grey and white marbled moonstone necklace to Mist and instructed her to leave.

Chapter Five

Coralee slept soundly through the night. She awoke to the cry of seagulls and the brisk sea breeze fluttering her curtains. She busied herself by making breakfast and cleaning the kitchen, all the while trying to make sense of the events from the night before.

It just couldn't be, thought Coralee, *maybe I imagined it or had a vivid daydream.*

But the events from the night before haunted her. She couldn't understand it because it did not make sense. She felt something was calling her back to where she stood on the seashore last night. The feeling was extraordinarily strong. She finally resigned herself to once more climb down the cliff wall before her grandfather returned that afternoon.

Maybe if I see things in the light of day it will all make sense, she reasoned.

In the morning light, the sea twinkled like a blanket of diamonds. Coralee carefully scaled down the rock face until she stepped off the rocks and onto the black sand beach. The tiny cove looked peaceful and serene, but something felt odd. She felt like someone, or something, was watching her.

Coralee tried to calm down by telling herself it was just her vivid imagination when she heard a girl's voice, not with her ears, but with her mind. She froze in place and tried to focus on the sound. The waves coming ashore made it difficult. The voice became louder; the voice was that of a girl sending her a message.

"My name is Mist; you came to my aid last night. I am a merling, a young mermaid of the Nereus Pod. I came to repay your kindness. It is our way."

Coralee spun around but saw no one.

"You cannot see me, though I am near. I speak to you telepathically; it is one of my powers. Go to the large grey boulder on the other side of the cove. There you will find a necklace with a stone attached."

Coralee followed Mist's instructions and located the necklace. It was a grey and white marbled stone attached to a long piece of fishing twine.

"This necklace I give to you contains a moonstone that has magical powers. If ever you are in danger, near or on the sea, simply grasp the moonstone in the palm of your hand and repeat this chant: 'Mermaids of Nereus, hear my plea, I am in peril, please come save me.' When the stone turns teal, you will know we have heard you and we will render you help. But beware, if you speak of the stone or what you have seen, a fatal curse will befall you."

"Why would you help me? It is told that mermaids are evil sorcerers who lure men through the depths of the sea to their doom?" questioned Coralee.

"Those are the Sirens, an evil pod of mermaids. We are the Nereus. We are healers; we protect the seas' rich bounties; we live in peace with nature. This moonstone is a sacred gift bestowed upon but few humans. Guard it carefully and keep it with you always. Do not forget what I have told you. Farewell, Coralee."

Coralee heard a tail fluke hitting the water and then there was silence. Mystified, she took the necklace and tied it around her neck. It was long enough to be disguised by tucking it into her shirt.

"Even if I did tell someone, they would never believe me," chuckled Coralee.

She climbed back up the cliff to the lighthouse and prepared to start painting the inside of the cottage.

"I think I'll paint Grandpa's room first since he is still in town. I need to focus on something else," she sighed. "The morning's events were a bit overwhelming."

The Sea Goddess, Kleenah, called a mandatory meeting of all the members of the Nereus pod.

"I have received word from our warriors that the Sirens are starting to assemble. Until further notice all Nereids are restricted to quarters. We have heightened our patrols. This may be our last chance to finally defeat this pod of Sirens that has plagued us for so long. As soon as I receive intel as to their exact assembly point, I will then call upon all the mermaids to gather so we may join our powers to aide our warriors in their battle to defeat the Sirens. Be forewarned! We are in for turbulent seas."

Chapter Six

Rigger was full of good cheer when he returned to the lighthouse late in the afternoon.

"Ahoy, mate!" Rigger called out to Coralee. "So, what have you been doing to keep yourself busy while I was away?"

Oh, if only I could tell him, thought Coralee.

"I've started painting the inside of the cottage. I just finished your bedroom, Grandpa."

"You didn't paint it pink, did ya?" joked Rigger.

"No, Grandpa, the paint color is 'ocean breeze,' come look for yourself."

Coralee had the walls painted and the furniture back in place. A white quilt that had a navy-blue compass sewn in the center covered the bed. There was a white cable-knit afghan on the old rocking chair. She even added a few decorative nautical items to the room to make it even cozier.

"Well, I'll be hornswoggled! It looks absolutely beautiful, Coralee. I hardly recognize it as my room."

"How's the painting and repair work coming on the outside of the cottage?" inquired Coralee.

"Everything is patched. I've got the shutters painted—just need to whitewash

the façade."

"I bet I get done painting the inside before you finish painting the outside," quipped Coralee.

"I'll take that bet," grinned Rigger. "The loser buys the winner lunch at the Seadog Café."

"You're on, Grandpa."

Over the course of the next week, Coralee completed painting the inside of the cottage, adding decorative nautical touches here and there. The cottage seemed to spring to life once again. It had a fresh, airy feel to it. She was so pleased with how it turned out.

"I think I won the bet," she muttered to herself.

Outside the cottage, Rigger was busy hanging up the bright red shutters on the windows. The cottage's newly painted white façade seemed to glisten in the sunlight. It stood proudly upon the grey rocks of Silver Wing Point.

"Hey, guess what?!" exclaimed Coralee. "I won the bet!"

"I finished painting before you," replied Rigger.

"The job isn't complete until all the shutters are up, so I won!" rejoiced Coralee.

"OK, you got me there, lunch is on me tomorrow."

The next morning at breakfast Rigger was checking the weather forecast.

"Hey, there's a full moon tonight, and the weather's going to be calm and clear. It will be a great night to go fishing. You know you catch the biggest fish at night, Coralee."

Coralee smiled; it seemed as if the sea flowed through Grandpa's veins.

"What about the lunch you owe me?" reminded Coralee.

"Well, I was thinkin', you drive me down to the Seadog Café and we'll have lunch. Then I'll do some work on the *Ole Scallywag* and get her ready for launch this evening. I'll be returning to the lagoon in the wee hours of the morning, so I'll just spend the night on the *Ole Scallywag*. You can fetch me in the morning."

"OK," said Coralee, "I think I'll spend my evening finishing up my mystery novel."

Rigger loaded the trawler with his fishing gear and started her up.

She still purrs like a kitten, thought Rigger.

Chapter Seven

As Rigger guided the *Ole Scallywag* out of port, memories flooded back to an earlier time, back to his maiden voyage with her. He was a novice fisherman headed out on a moonlit night at dusk for fishing, much like this evening.

In the wee hours of the morning as he was returning to the lagoon, he remembered how he'd heard what sounded like a large aquatic animal in distress. Upon searching the sea with his spotlight, he could see what looked like a tail fin caught in discarded fishing net. How he hated irresponsible fishermen! He turned the trawler and gently inched closer for a better look.

The young mermaid, Kleenah, was being chased by a predator wolffish. Swimming for her life as fast as she could, she successfully outmaneuvered the predator and inadvertently swam right into a ghost fishing net, abandoned by a careless fisherman. In her panicked thrashing to set herself free, she only tangled herself up more. In the distance she heard the motor of a fishing vessel approach. She feared for her life.

Rigger remembered he cut the engine and drifted forward. Searching again with his spotlight, he located the creature in distress, forty-five degrees off his port bow. It was a risk to get in the water with a panicked marine animal, but he could not let it suffer either. He grabbed his switchblade and dove into the dark sea. He grabbed sections of the fishing net and worked quickly to cut it free. With the last cut of the switchblade, the creature swam away swiftly. As it darted through the water, he recalled he noticed the scales did not look like any fish he had ever encountered, and there seemed to be glimmers of gold from the dorsal fin.

Rigger smiled as he recalled that chapter of his youth. He pushed the throttle forward and sped through the water. With one hand on the helm, he touched the choker he always wore around his neck and thought of how this unknown sea creature had revealed herself to him a week later on a similar nocturnal fishing trip.

Without saying a word, she threw the choker necklace on the stern of the trawler. She said her name was Kleenah and she communicated to him the relevance of the moonstone necklace, her way of thanking him for saving her life. As the *Ole Scallywag's* engines hummed through the dark waters, Rigger pondered, *what was that chant she taught me?*

* * *

A Nereus scout warrior secretly followed a couple of merling Sirens. His powers allowed him to read their thoughts. They were headed to Flaming Skull Ridge near a large volcanic sea chimney, eagerly anticipating the message they would receive from their Siren leader. Now the warrior knew the location where the Sirens would gather to perform their infernal sorcery. They would, no doubt, conjure up horrific sea storms causing shipwrecks and drownings. He quickly reported this the Sea God Cronus, who was also patrolling the region. Cronus directed him to relay his message to Kleenah at once. Cronus then readied his fellow warriors for battle.

* * *

Rigger set anchor at one of his favorite fishing spots. He cut the engine, let out his fishing lines, then settled back in his captain's chair and enjoyed the moonlit sea.

After a few hours the wind started to pick up, the sea became choppy, and the sky was turning dark.

What's this all about? he wondered. *This wasn't in the forecast.*

He went below deck and got his rain slicker on, and then returned and started pulling in his fishing lines. The weather worsened, and water came gushing down like a waterfall. The merciless winds caused enormous waves to crash into the hull of the *Ole Scallywag.*

This was a monster storm, and not one Rigger wanted to be a part of. After several attempts he got the engines started. He weighed anchor and pushed the throttle all the way forward. The waves were erupting like lava coming from a raging volcano. Sheets of rain were pouring down. Rigger struggled to maintain control of the vessel. His instrument panel went dark, and he lost radio communication. The angry sea tossed the *Ole Scallywag* like a cork.

Rigger became disoriented; he wasn't sure he was still on course for Lost Lily Lagoon. It was taking all his strength to keep control of the vessel. He feared he was losing the battle when suddenly he remembered the moonstone choker. He grabbed the necklace and ripped it from his neck, holding the moonstone in the palm of his hand as he recited the mermaid's incantation over and over.

"Gale force winds, please rescind; fog and mist, please desist; on this ship lay mermaid hands, and guide me safely back to land!"

* * *

The raging storm was beginning to roll into Silver Wing Point. Coralee checked the lighthouse lanterns and then jumped in her truck and quickly drove to Lost Lily Lagoon to see if her grandpa had returned.

She ran through the rain and into the Seadog Café, "Dorsea, have you heard from Grandpa?"

"The storm has knocked out the short-wave radio. Your grandfather is an excellent sailor. If anyone can get through this storm he can."

Not this storm, thought Coralee, *he needs help.*

Coralee ran back to her truck through sheets of rain. She pulled the moonstone necklace out of her shirt and began repeating the incantation Mist told her.

Eventually the stone turned teal, and she heard Mist's voice.

"Coralee, how can I help you?"

"My grandfather is lost in this storm. Please find him and render him aid."

"I will inform the mermaids; we will do our best to assist your grandfather."

With that the stone turned back to grey.

Chapter Eight

The Nereus warriors were en route to engage in battle with the Sirens. Kleenah called all her mermaids to the throne room where a large golden pearl stood on a pedestal in the center of the room. The mermaids encircled the pedestal and placed their hands upon the pearl. They began singing an incantation, causing the powerful energy of the pearl to cast bright beams of golden light throughout the room.

As the power of the pearl grew to peak intensity, Kleenah placed her hand upon the top of the pearl to draw in the immense wealth of power generated by the mermaids. She then telepathically conveyed this huge beam of energy to her warriors, to empower and shield them from the witchcraft of the Sirens.

Kleenah was receiving a telepathic message from a young fisherman she encountered years ago. He was lost in this storm and needed help.

* * *

Just then, Mist entered the throne room to convey the message she received from Coralee. Kleenah was clairvoyant and could see the young girl crying for her grandfather, and an older man barely staying afloat in the storm.

"They are of the same family," deciphered Kleenah. "Quickly, mermaids, we must locate this fisherman. He can't hold off this storm much longer—time is of the essence!"

* * *

In the storm's fury, Rigger could hardly maintain his grip on the helm; his fingers had turned ice cold. He continued repeating the mermaid's chant repeatedly, when he noticed a teal glow emitting from the fingers of his left hand.

"Kleenah is coming!" Rigger sighed in relief, "If I can just hold on just a bit longer."

At top speed, the mermaids swam as fast as marlin, although the tempestuous sea hampered their speed. Kleenah's vision gave her his location.

"I've located him. Hurry, he has no strength left!"

With their combined supernatural strength and powers, they turned the trawler towards Lost Lily Lagoon to guide it home.

Rigger was slumped over the helm, "Kleenah," he spoke in a weak voice.

"Yes, Rigger, I am here. We're going to take you safely back to port."

Chapter Nine

Cronus was pleased. The powers of the golden pearl had shielded his warriors from the Sirens' merciless sorcery, allowing them the tactical edge to capture them. The leader of the Sirens was restrained and brought forward to Cronus.

"Your days of terrorizing the sea with your witchcraft and sorcery are over," Cronus stated harshly. "The Sirens will be stripped of all their powers, and I will cast a punishment most deserving upon you. You will all be transformed into huge, flat, ugly Mola Molas—a fish with no purpose but to float aimlessly throughout the seas."

Cronus then wielded his all-powerful trident upon the Sirens and magically they turned into Mola Molas.

Kleenah instructed Mist to telepath Coralee that her grandfather was in the lagoon. They could go no farther as dawn was breaking and they could not be seen. Mist did as she was instructed and sent the message to her.

* * *

Coralee was sitting in the back booth of the café with the stone tightly gripped in her hands. The stone turned teal, and she heard Mist relay the message to send someone to pull her grandfather's trawler into port.

"Coralee, we cast a spell to put your grandfather to sleep while we escorted him home. Do not worry; he weathered the storm. He will awaken as soon as the sun rises."

"Thank you, Mist, I am forever grateful. Be assured, your secrets of the sea are forever safe with me."

She tucked her moonstone necklace back under her shirt and ran to the docks.

Once the trawler had been pulled into port, Coralee went aboard the *Ole Scallywag* to find her grandfather sitting in the captain's chair, dazed but otherwise okay. His choker necklace was hanging from his fingertips. As she reached to grab it, she noticed the stone in the center was the exact stone she wore around her neck, a moonstone.

"Well, it seems grandfather has some secrets of his own," smiled Coralee.

Grandfather had never spoke of the mermaid, Kleenah, and Coralee never spoke of her mermaid, Mist, but somehow, she knew he had had a previous encounter with one of them.

Chapter Ten

The summer was ending, and the lighthouse renovation was complete. Coralee had to return home to prepare for the next school year, but this was a summer she would never forget. The bond between her and her grandfather had only grown stronger.

Rigger loaded the back of her truck with her suitcases. He wasn't much for mushy goodbyes. Coralee said "goodbye," gave her grandpa a big hug, and got into the truck.

Rigger waved goodbye and yelled, "May you have fair winds whilst following the seas!"

Coralee had to laugh as she waved and drove away thinking, *he really does have the sea running through his veins!*

Author bio

Cindy Rand started writing children's literature quite by accident. After she met a lovely elderly couple recently relocated to an Assistant Living facility, she was asked by their daughter to keep an eye on them for the month she would be preparing their house for sale. To brighten their day, Cindy wrote a children's story with them as the main characters. Unbeknownst to Cindy, the story was passed around the facility with rave reviews. With all the positive reception, she decided to pursue writing and bring the joy of reading to children of all ages, as well as to those adults who still enjoy a fun, exciting children's story.

CPSIA information can be obtained
at www.ICGtesting.com
Printed in the USA
BVHW011501230623
666300BV00007B/295